Pitch Dark

Robert Dodds

A & C Black • London

For Eleanor Jones – "football mad."

First published 2012 by A & C Black
an imprint of Bloomsbury Publishing Plc
50 Bedford Square London WC1B 3DP

www.acblack.com

Text copyright © 2012 Robert Dodds
Illustrations copyright © 2012 Mike Lacey

ISBN 978-1-4081-5573-8

A CIP catalogue for this book is available from the British Library.

recommended by

www.catchup.org

Catch Up is a not-for-profit charity
which aims to address the problem of
underachievement that has its roots in
literacy and numeracy difficulties.

Pitch Dark

Contents

Chapter 1

New Start

"Sorry, we've already got a goalie," said
Steven.

David nodded, trying not to look too sad.

Steven was captain of the school team.
He was not being unkind. He was just telling
it how it was.

Steven could see how upset David was,
even though David tried to hide it.

"Maybe we could give you a try-out
one lunch break anyway?" Steven went on.
"Then we could see if you were any good.
I don't think our goalie, Nick, would mind
that."

"Thanks," said David, as Steven gave him
a thumbs-up sign and walked away.

* * *

David was finding it hard to fit in at his new school. He missed his old friends, but most of all he missed being goalie in his old school's football team.

Every day after school David took a short cut to get home. The short cut took him through a part of town where all the shops and houses were boarded up, and the streets were empty. It was like a ghost town.

Right in the heart of this area was an old football stadium.

There were holes in the fence around it,
and David always cut across the pitch on his
way home.

It looked like it had once been a really
smart stadium. There was a proper stand with
terraces at the front and seating higher up, but
the roof now sagged and had holes in it.

A big sign in red paint said, "Danger of
Death! Keep Out!"

On the pitch itself, there were weeds
everywhere, but you could just make out some
faint white lines on the ground. The goal
posts were bent, and the nets hung like broken
cobwebs from the crossbars.

David liked to stand in goal at one end of the pitch for a few moments each evening. He pretended he could hear the roar of the crowd as he made a brilliant save.

Chapter 2

Stadium Scare

One afternoon in November, David was going home as usual through the empty stadium.

The old football pitch seemed a bit scary now that the nights were getting darker. There were street-lights at the far end, but they did not give out much light. Half the pitch was in darkness, and there was no light at all under the roof of the stand.

David had a strange feeling that there was an invisible crowd sitting there, watching him.

He started to jog quickly, to get across the pitch as soon as he could.

Then he saw something right on the centre spot.

It was a football, old, but in quite good condition.

David looked around, but saw no-one. Then he backed up, took a short run, and kicked the ball hard. It flew off into the darkness at the end of the field.

David sighed.

If only he had some team-mates to kick around with.

Then he heard the sound of a kick, and the ball came flying back up the pitch towards him. It rolled to a stop right by his feet.

He stared into the gloom.

"Hello?" he called out.

"Hello? Hello? Hello?" came the echoes from the stand.

But there was no reply from whoever had kicked the ball back to him.

The hairs stood up on the back of David's neck. But he wanted to find out who had kicked the ball, so he dribbled it slowly up the pitch towards the darkness.

Chapter 3

A Stranger in
the Stand

David got right up to the goalposts at the
dark end of the pitch, but there was no one to
be seen.

A cold gust of wind blew against his face and made him shiver. The wind pulled at the goal nets and rattled the broken roof of the stand.

Suddenly, he saw something that made him jump. Up there, in the darkness under the roof, he could just make out a seated man, staring down at him.

David heard a horrible squealing noise and the man started to move, but without standing up. It was weird and scary, until David realised that the man was in a wheelchair, and the squealing noise was made by the wheels.

How on earth had the man got up there in a wheelchair?

Suddenly, David just wanted to get away.

He left the football where it was, and ran down the pitch to the gap in the fence. He crawled through, and didn't stop running until he came back to a part of town where there were cars and buses and people again.

Only then did he slow down, but his heart was still pounding.

As David walked the final part of his way home, he felt a little bit foolish. It must have been somebody having a bit of fun, kicking the ball to him and then hiding.

He should have stuck around for longer. Maybe he should have tried to speak to the man in the wheelchair. He'd probably looked stupid, suddenly running off like that.

Anyway, he would have to cross the football pitch on his way home from school again tomorrow. With a bit of luck, maybe this time he would meet the mysterious footballer, and he'd have someone to kick around with after all.

Chapter 4

Team Tryout

At lunch break the next day Steven came over to talk to David.

"Hey David," Steven said.

"Hi," said David.

"Do you want to come and stand in goal on the field?" asked Steven. "I've got some of the guys ready to practise penalty shots."

David felt nervous, but this was his chance to show Steven what he could do.

"Okay – I'll just get my trainers out of my locker," he said.

"Great," said Steven. "See you there."

* * *

When David got to the field, someone was already in goal, defending shots from Steven and four other boys.

As David walked up, the goalie made a brilliant save, stopping a high curving ball into the corner.

"Nick!" Steven called out, "Take a rest and let David have a go!"

Nick nodded, and moved around to the back of the net, giving David a long, hard look.

"You always been a goalie?" Nick asked David, as the first boy took aim with a shot.

David was put off by the question and the ball whizzed past him. It was a low shot, about halfway between him and the goalpost, and he should have stopped it easily.

"I've been the goalie for our team for two years now," said Nick.

Steven was next to take a shot at the goal. Just as he started his run at the ball, Nick said to David, "I saw you going into the old football ground last night."

David had never seen anyone else in that part of town. He was too surprised to move as Steven's shot flew past his left ear and into the net.

"That used to be the town ground, before the tragedy," said Nick.

"What tragedy?" said David, but at that moment the next shot came straight towards him.

He got his hands to the ball, but it slipped from his grasp and dribbled over the line.

"Ten years ago, it was," Nick went on. "The whole team was wiped out."

"How?" David said, not sure whether to believe this strange story.

"Road accident. The team bus went off a motorway bridge. Only one of them survived. He was the team coach – and he was the goalkeeper too," Nick went on.

Steven was getting ready for another shot at goal.

"He ended up in a wheelchair," Nick said.

David half turned in surprise to look at Nick just as Steven's shot came speeding towards the goal. It hit David on the side of his head, and came to rest in the net behind him.

"Ow!" cried David.

"Oh dear," Nick said. "Never mind, eh?"

Steven walked up to the goal. The other boys came closer too, to hear what he was going to say.

"Okay, David," Steven said. "Er... I'll tell you what, you can be the reserve keeper if ever Nick can't make it to a game."

All the boys laughed, and David felt himself turning red.

"I've never missed a match in two years," said Nick as he took his place on the goal line.

Chapter 5

Night Practice

David felt very low as he made his way home that evening. Before going into the old football ground, he looked around to see if Nick was spying on him again.

As he walked across the pitch, David had the feeling he was being watched. He stared into the stand, but there was no one there.

Then he looked along the pitch and nearly jumped out of his skin.

There was the man in the wheelchair again. This time he was sitting right in the goal-mouth, at the dark end of the ground.

Nick's story came back into David's mind. Surely this must be the old coach and goalkeeper, still hanging about the ground and remembering the days when it was filled with action and the noise of the crowd.

The man raised an arm and waved. David walked towards him, and saw that the old football was by the man's feet.

"I've seen you a few times, young man," the stranger said. His voice was a croaky whisper, and his face was hidden under an old cap. His skin looked grey and bloodless, but his eyes were shining in the darkness.

"What's your name, lad?" the man croaked.

"I'm David."

"You're a keen footballer, aren't you, David?" the man said.

"Yes, I am."

"What position do you play?"

"I'm a goalie."

The man's head lifted and his eyes glinted. "A goalie!" he said. "That's the best job in the game! Do you want to defend a few shots in goal now?"

David stared at the man. Was he mad? Who was going to take the shots?

"Oh, I can't kick a ball any more," the strange man said with a laugh, "but you'll find I can throw one pretty hard!"

David put down his school bag at the side of the goalposts and took up his position, while the man wheeled himself and the ball to the penalty spot.

As soon as he got there, he hurled the ball at the goal.

David was taken by surprise by the power of the throw, but he quickly moved across the goal line to catch the ball.

"Well done, David!" the man said. "Send it back!"

David kicked the ball back to the man, who leaned over to scoop it up.

In an instant it was flying back towards the goal-mouth, this time up into the far corner. David threw himself sideways and managed to punch the ball away. His goalkeeping was back on form now that he didn't have Nick distracting him.

The man gave him about a dozen shots, and he saved all but one of them.

"Well, David, you clearly know what you're doing," the man said at last. "I think Sandy, the captain, would be happy with that."

"Who?" David said.

"Sandy. He's a super captain, David. A striker – he leads from the front. But there's a strong defence too. Young Chris Jones and Mike Cooper are brilliant tacklers. And they'll mark their men for you. No worries about that. The opposition strikers won't get any easy shots in the penalty box!"

David grew more and more confused. Then he realised that the man was talking about the town's football team. They were all dead, but he spoke as if they were still alive.

The poor guy! The tragic crash that had killed all his team-mates must have driven him mad.

"Let me tell you about our game against Camford," the man said. "That was a cracker…"

"Er… I think my mum will have tea on the table by now," said David quickly. He felt sorry for the strange man, but he also wanted an excuse to get away.

The man gave David a long hard look, but he didn't say another word.

"Well, goodbye then," David said and ran off. When he got to the gap in the fence, he turned to wave goodbye. But the man was nowhere to be seen.

Chapter 6

The Mistake

A ball of paper flew through the air and hit David on the side of the head.

"Goal!" someone shouted, and lots of people laughed.

It was the gap between lessons, and there was no teacher in the room so things were getting a little noisy.

David looked around to see who had thrown the ball of paper. Then he saw Nick grinning.

Nick called out, "Still sneaking into the old football stadium for a bit of practice?"

David wondered how Nick knew what he did after school. But he didn't want to make an enemy of Nick, so he got up from his desk and went over to talk to him.

"I did go into the old ground, yes," he said quietly.

He knew that Steven was listening, as well as some of the other boys in the football team.

"And when I was in there, I met the goalie of the old town team," David went on.

Nick's face suddenly went white, and he stared back at David.

"What?" he said.

"The old goalkeeper – the one in a wheelchair," said David.

Now Nick looked like he was going to cry. He gave David a shove and stormed out of the classroom.

David stared after him. What was going on?

"You jerk!" said Steven crossly, "Making up a story like that."

"What?" asked David.

"You know very well," Steven went on. "The goalkeeper of the old town team was Nick's dad!"

David went bright red.

"I didn't know that, actually," David said. "Anyway, what's wrong with saying I met Nick's dad?"

"You know!" said Steven, angrily.

"I don't know," David said, starting to feel angry himself.

Steven looked at David and spoke slowly.

"Nick's dad is dead."

David felt as if the floor had dropped from under him.

"But…" he said, "…Nick told me the goalie survived the crash. He said that he was in a wheelchair…"

"True," Steven said, cutting in, "but he died last year from a heart attack."

David just stared at him.

"You can forget about being reserve goalie for the team," Steven went on, "and if you make up any more nasty lies, you'll be sorry."

Just then, the teacher came into the room.

David sat down. His brain was buzzing. Who was the man he'd met in the wheelchair, who seemed to know all about the old football team?

And how on earth was he going to make Nick believe he hadn't meant to upset him?

Chapter 7

Keep Out!

After school David made his way home across the old football pitch.

The sky was dark and the wind was howling. The metal roof of the old stand rattled violently.

Over the noise of the wind, he could hear his name being called.

"David! David!"

He looked up.

There, high up in the stand, was the man
in the wheelchair, waving at him.

Once again, David wondered how he had
got there.

"David! Come up here!" the man called.

David felt anger well up inside him.

This guy and his crazy stories had caused all the trouble at school. He was the reason why Nick was so upset, and why David would never get a chance to play for the school team.

In a rush, David stepped over the "Danger of Death! Keep Out!" sign, which had blown over, and started to climb up into the stand.

"What's your name?" he shouted, as he got close to the man. "Who are you?"

The man's head lifted, and his eyes shone with a strange light under the rim of his cap.

David suddenly felt afraid and came to a dead stop.

There was a terrible tearing noise above him. He looked up quickly, and let out a cry of horror. A huge part of the old iron roof had come loose, and was falling towards him like an axe.

A wave of pain tore through his whole body. Then darkness took him, and everything went black.

Chapter 8

Making The Team

David opened his eyes. He was lying on the ground, and above him he could see the crossbar of a goal.

Slowly, he moved his arms. There was no pain.

How could that be? Surely he must be hurt?

He stood up carefully, and looked about him, very confused. He remembered climbing into the stand, and the falling roof…

The faint light from the far off street-lights cast a shadow of the goalposts onto the grass in front of him. He waved his arms a little, staring at the ground.

Where was his own shadow?

Then David heard a noise coming from the darkness at the end of the pitch.

It was the sound of footballers running, and calling to each other. He heard a ball being kicked. Suddenly, the ball curved towards him out of the blackness, and without thinking, he reached out and caught it.

He stood looking at the ball in his hands, feeling suddenly very afraid, and very alone.

When he looked up again, David could just make out some shadowy figures in the darkness in front of him. They were standing on the edge of the penalty box, facing him.

Then David heard a squealing sound and the man in the wheelchair came into view at the edge of the pitch.

With a sinking feeling of horror, David suddenly understood.

This *was* Nick's dad! Nick's dead dad…
"Come on, David!" the man called out.
"Throw the ball back to the lads! You're one
of the team now! Come on, look lively!"

Dead Wood

Holly's family move to the old house so
her dad can do his job: bulldozing the ancient
trees to make way for a housing estate. But
there's something haunting the old house.
Something old, and angry, that doesn't want
the trees cut down. Something *alive*...

ISBN 978-1-4081-6335-1
RRP £5.99

Drawing a Veil

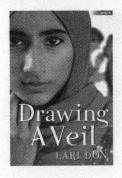

Ellie and Amina are best friends. But when
Amina decides to start wearing the hijab, it
attracts the attention of the bullies. Does it
matter if best friends have different beliefs?
A thought-provoking story about friendship,
culture and modern life.

ISBN 978-1-4081-5559-2
RRP £5.99

Zero to Hero

Will is football mad, but he's the shortest boy in the year, and one of the slowest. He knows his skills at passing and ball control could make up for his lack of size, but the team coach is looking for fast players. Will he ever get a chance to show what he can do?

ISBN 978-1-4081-5560-8
RRP £5.99